BY

LORRAINE JONES-WHITFIELD

© 2018 by Lorraine Jones-Whitfield

All rights reserved. This book or any portion thereof may not be reproduced or used in any manner whatsoever without the express written permission of the publisher except for the use of brief quotations in a book review.

Printed in the United States of America

ISBN: 978-0-578-41577-2

First Edition

10 9 8 7 6 5 4 3 2 1

Table of Contents

Acknowledgements 5
Introduction 7
Avoid Anger 9
Attitude Is Altitude. 10
Believe in Yourself 11
You Are Beauty-Full. 12
Being Bold. 13
Committed to the Call. 14
Confidently Confident. 15
Be Courageous 16
Courage Is Being Fearless 17
Carefully Created 18
Compassion Is Caring 19
Empowered by God 20
Faithing It 21
Forgiveness Is Freedom 22
Family Oriented 23
God's Word 24
Grace Is Amazing. 25
Honesty Is Best 26
Honor (Roll) 27
Hope-Full 28
Integrity Is Key 29
Joy Unspeakable 30

Love 31

Obedience 32

Praise Is What We Do 33

Be Passionate 34

Peer Pressure 35

Perseverance 36

Prayer — the Game Changer 37

Respect 38

Self-Control 39

Live Selflessly 40

Thankfulness 41

Trust Him 42

Values 43

Wisdom 44

About the Author 45

Acknowledgements

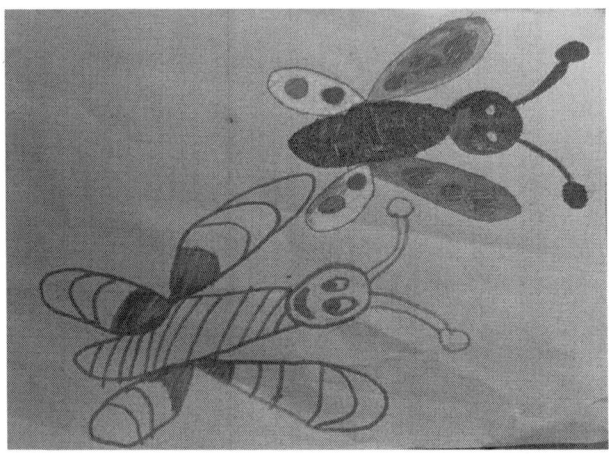

To Lydia Williams, a creative young lady who has some issues in her life, drew this butterfly. I'm glad you finished in in time for this book. Butterflies are one of my favorite insects. They represent my transformation — from childhood to adulthood.

To my grandchildren — Jordan, Hayden, Quincy, Olive, Kilea, Gabriel, King, Josiah, Eliza, Amy, Jocelyn, Jaeden, Alberto, and Janelle—as well as to all the other children who have come into my life.

Introduction

Faith is having confidence in something or someone even though you don't know what will happen. You can have faith in your study habits to help you ace a test, faith in your soccer skills to put you in a position to score a goal, or faith in your friends to help you when you need it. Faith is believing in something without seeing it happen first.

This journal is about helping you to have faith in God. He has everything under control, and if we don't doubt, we will always win. Challenges and storms may arise, but, in the mist of them, we can always look back at God's Word and remember His promises. Romans 8:28 says, "And we know that in all things God works for the good of those who love him, who have been called according to his purpose" (NIV).

Hopefully in reading through this journal and doing the writing exercises, you will see that your faith will move God. When you faith it, God gives you the strength to stand up in hard times or to change areas of your life that are hard for you to change. Your faith will give you the confidence that God can help and heal. Your faith must embrace the Word of God. "Now faith is the substance of things hoped for, the evidence of things not seen" (Hebrews 11:1 KJV).

As you journal, you'll learn bits and pieces of God's Word, and I hope it will increase your faith. You must understand that this faith walk is real and very important. Without faith, it's impossible to please God (Hebrews 11:6). It's not about your church. You may have a big church and a fun youth group, but without faith, you have nothing. God wants you to trust Him first before anyone else. When you do, that's when your life will begin to change. That's faithing it.

How to Use Your Journal

As you begin this journal, you may need a few things—your Bible, pens or pencils, and markers. Let's get started:

1. **Gather your journaling/writing supplies and pray**
   Get your favorite pens or pencils and get ready to write and take notes from your Bible or from your thoughts. As you read and write, ask God to reveal what he wants you to learn from His Word today.

2. **Personalize your journal**
   Use stickers and markers to add decoration. Use different colored pens, or colored pencils to color code your notes.

3. **Choose a time**
   When it comes to studying your Bible, time matters. Try before or after school or right before bed.

4. **Get started**
   Open you journal and dive in. Draw on your page, color, and create, but most of all, *faith it*!

Avoid Anger

"But now you must put them all away: anger, wrath, malice, slander, and obscene talk from your mouth."

Colossians 3:8 (ESV)

According to the dictionary, anger is a strong feeling of annoyance that can be caused by a disappointment. It is almost a resentment toward something.

Because we are God's children, we must set our minds on God and not the things other children do. We must believe that God can change every situation.

Try to choose your friends wisely and listen to your parents. Do not allow others to influence your thoughts. Believe in yourself and remember that anger is a choice. God's Word says to put off anger, put on a meek and humble spirit, and be kind to one another (Colossians 3:8–14). You will run into situations that you will not be able to change, but you still have control over how you respond.

I will:

_____
_____
_____
_____
_____
_____
_____
_____
_____
_____
_____
_____

Attitude Is Altitude

"And I say unto you, Ask, and it shall be given you; seek, and ye shall find; knock, and it shall be opened unto you."

Luke 11:9 (KJV)

"Attitude" is a way of looking at things.

At times, people might say to you, "Watch your attitude." You may respond, "I don't have an attitude." However, "attitude" is the way we look at things and react to situations. I have often told my granddaughter to change her attitude, but she could never realize when she had a bad attitude. I had to reassure her that God loves her. No matter what you are dealing with, God loves you, and He will always be there for you. Even when our lives seem stressful and our situations seem overwhelming, we must remember that our attitude determines our altitude.

God will provide for you. He knows everything you go through and will guide you every step of the way. Something may seem very hard but trust Him instead of getting an attitude. He will redeem your mistakes, and all things will work together for your good (Romans 8:28). Just know that His Word is right.

Set aside five minutes to pray for God's guidance about a situation that angers you. Memorize a calming Bible verse, such as Psalm 121:1 — "I lift up my eyes to the mountains — where does my help come from?"

I will:

_____
_____
_____
_____
_____
_____
_____

Believe in Yourself

"I can do all things through Christ who strengthens me."

Philippians 4:13 (NKJV)

Believe in yourself because no one can do what you were meant to do better than you can. It may be hard to believe in yourself if you have been told you will never be anything. However, remember that in God's eyes, you are everything.

Look at all the beauty inside you. Make a list of your past accomplishments. This will help you start believing in yourself. Write everything down — from the smallest thing to the greatest. Next, talk to people who care about and love you. Find a reason to believe in yourself. Finally, set some goals for yourself and reflect on your plan and purpose each day.

Affirm yourself and give yourself a reason to smile. Through all your good times and bad times, believe that God is always with you and will never leave you alone. Believe that He will share in your joy and hug you in your sadness. He will not leave you in times of disappointment because you believe in Him and believe that His Word is true.

I will:

_____
_____
_____
_____
_____
_____
_____
_____
_____

You Are Beauty-Full

"I praise you because I am fearfully and wonderfully made; your works are wonderful, I know that full well."

Psalm 139:14 (NIV)

"Beauty" is the quality of being physically attractive.

If you are a teen girl, you are probably always looking for ways to be stylish and get into the latest fashions. You may go through all the latest fashion magazines, watch all the fashion shows on television, and read many books.

However, do you realize that beauty has nothing to do with makeup and fashion but is about being a young woman who delights in God? Ask God to help you look to reality beneath the skin. Remember that all good things come from God. When you seek after God, you will be the most beautiful girl in the world.

If you are a young child, you, also, must realize that your beauty comes from God. Don't get caught up in the things of this world and become clouded by this worldly system. It's all right to look nice and pretty but try not to overdo it and take away from God's beauty. Say to God, "I praise you because I am fearfully and wonderfully made; your works are wonderful, I know that full well" (Psalm 139:14 NIV).

I will:

_____
_____
_____
_____
_____
_____
_____

Being Bold

"Have I not commanded you? Be strong and courageous. Do not be afraid; do not be discouraged, for the Lord your God will be with you wherever you go."

Joshua 1:9 (NIV)

Going to a new school and meeting new friends or starting a new job can be frightening. Many times, we just want to hide. Instead of asking God to give us boldness to do what is right and overcome our fear, we allow it to grow and grow. Before we know it, our fears have become giants in our lives.

Pray and ask God to take away your fear and equip you to conquer any situation. God has given you weapons to fight with and made you a warrior by teaching you to pray and be strong. Warriors do not run from fearful situations. They pray and march on in battle. Consider Ephesians 6:10 — "Be strong in the Lord and in his mighty power" (NIV).

I will:

_____
_____
_____
_____
_____
_____
_____
_____
_____
_____
_____
_____
_____

Committed to the Call

"Now flee from youthful lusts and pursue righteousness, faith, love, and peace, with those who call on the Lord from a pure heart."

2 Timothy 2:22 (NASB)

Commitment is dedicating yourself to a cause or activity. It's something you pledge. The word "commitment" may not be in the Bible, but Jesus shows us in many ways how we must be committed. Jesus was committed to His disciples (followers). We must love, trust, and obey Jesus above everything on earth — we must put Him first.

Matthew 16:24–26 says, "If anyone would come after me, let him deny himself and take up his cross and follow me" (ESV). Remember — when you're in school or playing sports or doing homework, your commitment does not depend on the honesty of others. Your friends may not agree with you or what you like to do. However, you must be dedicated to your purpose and the plan God has to help you reach your goals and dreams.

I will:

_____
_____
_____
_____
_____
_____
_____
_____
_____
_____
_____
_____
_____
_____

Confidently Confident

"Such confidence we have through Christ toward God."

2 Corinthians 3:4 (NASB)

What gives you confidence? At the end of each day, what fills your day with joy, security, or safety?

Parents often seek what they think is best for their children — the wisdom that will help them make the right choices and teach them how to get through tough situations.

It is so amazing to know that God has created you for His purpose and glory. Just think — there is no one exactly like you! No one has your exact smile, teeth, eye color, hair, or personality. You are created to be you! No one has your gifts, talents, or calling. God made you fearfully and wonderfully, so remain humble, seek God, and love those who are different from you because God created them, as well. You are your own uniqueness — God threw away the mold, so there is no one exactly like you!

I will:

_____
_____
_____
_____
_____
_____
_____
_____
_____
_____
_____
_____

Be Courageous

"Be of good courage, and he shall strengthen your heart, all ye that hope in the Lord."

Psalm 31:24 (KJV)

Be strong and have courage. Don't be afraid. You can find a lot of courageous people in the Bible — Daniel, Joshua, David, Ruth, Esther, and more. Read the first chapter of Ruth. She followed her mother-in-law, Naomi. Naomi travelled to a familiar place, but to Ruth, it was a new adventure. God told Joshua to take leadership when Moses died but not to be afraid, for God would be with him.

I often think of Kilea (my granddaughter), who has moved to many different states and countries because her dad is in the military. It was hard for her to leave her friends and family, but making new friends was easy for her. She was courageous and fearless but humble about each new adventure.

Sometimes we must trust God when we don't understand. Being a child, Kilea may not have understood why she had to move so much, but God has blessed her with a beautiful outcome. She trusted God, and He blessed her with victory. God's plan and future for His children is that we would be prosperous and successful (Joshua 1:8), unafraid because He will never leave us nor forsake us (Deuteronomy 31:6).

I will:

_____

_____

_____

_____

_____

_____

Courage Is Being Fearless

"Fear thou not; for I am with thee: be not dismayed; for I am thy God: I will strengthen thee; yea, I will help thee; yea, I will uphold thee with the right hand of my righteousness."

Isaiah 41:10 (KJV)

"Courage is doing what you're afraid to do. There can be no courage unless you're scared." — Edward Vernon Rickenbacker

Have you ever done something that you were scared to do, even though you knew it was right?

Courage is the ability to do something difficult, even when it may seem like a risk. As a kid, you build courage as you mature and take on challenges in your life. Courage is an important asset. When you find courage to do something new, you gain confidence. Having courage means you are brave enough to meet new challenges — new schools, new experiences, difficult situations, and maybe dangerous encounters. Courage is doing what you may be afraid to do. Walk by faith and not by sight (2 Corinthians 5:7). Learn to trust God every day.

I will:

_____
_____
_____
_____
_____
_____
_____
_____
_____
_____

Carefully Created

"I praise you because I am fearfully and wonderfully made; your works are wonderful, I know that full well."

Psalm 139:14 (NIV)

Creativity can come in many forms — acting, singing, dancing, playing an instrument, making art, etc. We could become doctors, lawyers, artists, photographers, gymnasts, musicians, and more. You are fearfully and wonderfully made, and God's works are marvelous (Psalm 139:14). He does not look at your faults because, in you, He sees perfection.

God created you for His glory and so that you would praise Him. He thinks you are wonderful. At school and at home, sometimes you may feel unworthy, and you may think you can't do anything right. However, you must see yourself as God sees you. God does not make mistakes. We are His masterpieces, and no pieces of art are identical. Each day, give yourself affirmation and encourage yourself in this journey.

I will:

_____
_____
_____
_____
_____
_____
_____
_____
_____
_____
_____
_____
_____

Compassion Is Caring

"Beloved, let us love one another: for love is of God; and everyone that loveth is born of God, and knoweth God."

1 John 4:7 (KJV)

Compassion is caring about others and offering them affection, generosity, and concern (putting yourself in their shoes). When we are compassionate, we have genuine feelings for other people's struggles, heartaches, or pain.

Compassion is a soft skill with real benefits. You don't have to like or agree with everything people do, but when you treat others with compassion, they are likely to treat you the same way. Compassion smooths out our interactions in the "real" world. When you use technology to communicate, you can't really feel or offer affection as much as you can in person.

Remember — there are real people on the other side of your screens. Jesus unwaveringly showed amazing compassion for the lost, the sick, and the entire world (Matthew 14:14). Let that inspire you to pray and seek a greater compassion toward the other kids in your school, in your neighborhood, in sports, on the playground, and everywhere. Ask God to teach you how to be compassionate toward your friends. Put yourself in their place when they are struggling, then ask what Jesus would do.

I will:

_____
_____
_____
_____
_____
_____
_____
_____

Empowered by God

"Have I not commanded you? Be strong and courageous. Do not be afraid; do not be discouraged, for the Lord your God will be with you wherever you go."

Joshua 1:9 (NIV)

When you fill your heart with God's love, good things will come out of your mouth. The best way to make sure this happens is to think about positive things in your mind and heart. "For out of the abundance of the heart the mouth speaks" (Matthew 12:34 NKJV).

Faithfully read your Bible and pray. Read one Bible verse before school, one after school, and one before bedtime, but pray always in your heart. Each day, be empowered by speaking affirmations to yourself, such as healing and comfort, and encourage yourself in tough times. When you are studying your homework, trust God to get you through. Keep your mind fixed on God's Word and good, positive things.

As a child, you need the encouragement of going outside and playing. You need to keep your mind fresh and productive. Play can restore the joy in your heart. The joy of the Lord is our strength! You are unique, and your uniqueness is your power. You can do all things through Christ who gives you the strength to do it (Philippians 4:13).

I will:

_____
_____
_____
_____
_____
_____
_____

Faithing It

"Now faith is the substance of things hoped for, the evidence of things not seen."

Hebrews 11:1 (KJV)

Being faithful can be a challenge at times. Hebrews 11:1 tells us that we need that "now faith" — the assurance of things hoped for, the conviction of things not seen. This reminds me of the time my family and I were at an amusement park and it started to pour down raining. By faith we had to find shelter, and it was hard because so many people needed it. God made a way. My grandson Hayden was wet but never complained, and my granddaughter Olive had the best seat in the house — a stroller. We had no doubt that God would take care of us in the storm. He protected us as we ran to the car to get out of the rain.

Going to school and even at an amusement park, faith can be tested. Maybe your faith is weak but remember — God will protect you on a school bus, in a car, and through every situation you may encounter. Fear not, for God will always be with you (Isaiah 41:10).

When you try to live out your faith but things in life seem hard, you may struggle to have confidence in God's protection. However, no matter what, know that God is there in any situation. Always keep your integrity, tell the truth, and especially be thankful for anything and everything.

School may get hard and your friends may disappoint you but remember that you have the confidence that God will bring you through. Positive thoughts will help you make positive choices, and before you know it, more friends will come along. God has a plan and purpose for you (Jeremiah 29:11).

I will: Faith it each day! I will trust God for the good things in life. I will walk by faith and not by sight — both at home and at school. I will trust God's Word.

I will:

_____

_____

_____

Forgiveness Is Freedom

"You, Lord, are forgiving and good, abounding in love to all who call to you."

Psalm 86:5 (NIV)

"Forgiveness" is an attitude or the act of forgiving someone.

It can be easy to stay mad with someone, but God's Word says that if we have sin in our hearts, He will not hear our prayers (Psalm 66:18). We must ask God to help us see the ones who have hurt us in the way He sees them. We must come to God and ask Him to help us forgive.

When we walk in forgiveness, God can turn our bad situations into good situations. Ask God to help you forgive someone who may have bullied you or a parent who hurt you or didn't raise you well. When you choose to forgive, you leap from pain to freedom.

Luke 6:37 says, "Forgive, and you will be forgiven" (NIV).

I will:

_____
_____
_____
_____
_____
_____
_____
_____
_____
_____
_____
_____
_____

Family Oriented

"Honor your father and your mother, so that you may live long in the land the Lord your God is giving you."

Exodus 20:12 (NIV)

As a kid, being a part of a family can be very important. Parents want their families under God's protection. As you grow and change, you will find yourself moving toward your friends and away from your family. However, spending time with your family should be the most important thing in your life because they will be there when everyone else is gone.

You probably do not like rules, and unless your parents make you, you may not follow their rules. However, your parents want what is best for you. The Bible tells parents to train up their children in the way they should go and to give their children a strong Christian foundation.

As preteens and teens, you want to be treated with more respect. For that to happen, you have to first honor and respect your parents. Honoring doesn't mean strict obedience, though you are to obey.

Honoring your parents is respecting your parent's, their rules, and their authority. It's staying calm when you disagree with their decisions, even after you have made your point.

I will:

_____
_____
_____
_____
_____
_____
_____
_____

God's Word

"In the beginning God created the heavens and the earth."

Genesis 1:1 (NIV)

The Bible is God's Word. Through reading God's Word, you can learn about wisdom, love, peace, joy, and more. God's Word will lead you to truth. There are so many promises in His Word that will help and encourage you every day.

To help you learn the Word of God, find a kids' Bible study or a youth group. Get together with a friend, listen to the Bible on your cell phone, and find time to read it daily. When you struggle in school, with family, with friends, or with anything else in life, God has something in His Word that will help you. You must search His Word until you find it.

If you walk around an amusement park and get lost, you will find that every road leads you back to the beginning. In a way, that's how God's Word is. Any struggle you may go through — whether it be on the playground, on the bus, during tests, or anywhere else — will lead you back to Him and teach you how to trust Him. If you hold the key of faith, God will unlock any door you need to go through. "Trust in the Lord with all your heart" (Proverbs 3:5 NIV).

I will:

_____
_____
_____
_____
_____
_____
_____
_____
_____

Grace Is Amazing

"But he said to me, 'My grace is sufficient for you, for my power is made perfect in weakness.'"

2 Corinthians 12:9 (NIV)

Grace is God's favor when we don't deserve it. How do you know what God wants you to do in your life? How can you make a decision without knowing if your decision will honor God's will?

Grace can be one of the hardest things for us to give. We easily forget that God gives us the same grace He wants us to give others. When it's hard to give grace, remember that God gave you grace.

"To each one of us grace was given according to the measure of Christ's gift" (Ephesians 4:7 NASB).

I will:
_____
_____
_____
_____
_____
_____
_____
_____
_____
_____
_____
_____
_____
_____
_____
_____
_____

Honesty Is Best

"My little children, let us not love in word, neither in tongue; but in deed, and in truth."

1 John 13:8 (KJV)

In whom or what do you put your trust? Many people seem to struggle with honesty — trusting that the truth is best in any situation. The Bible says, "You will know the truth, and the truth will make you free" (John 8:32 NASB). God's Word teaches us honesty. Lies lead to more lies. The more you lie, the easier it will be to lie. Soon you will find yourself in serious trouble.

Trust the Lord and do good. Always be honest. When you are honest, you live in freedom from lies and dishonesty. Telling the truth may have consequences — your friends may get angry, you may lose a friend —but it's much better to do what's right than to feel bad after telling a lie.

Be honest and live a free life as the Lord would have you to live. Pray each day that the Lord will keep you honest. Speak the truth from your heart so you can enjoy the presence of God (Psalm 15:1–2). In humility, ask God's forgiveness for the times you have not been entirely honest.

I will:
_____
_____
_____
_____
_____
_____
_____
_____
_____
_____
_____

Honor (Roll)

"Honor your father and your mother, as the Lord your God commanded you, that your days may be long, and that it may go well with you in the land that the Lord your God is giving you."

Deuteronomy 5:16 (ESV)

Romans 12:10 says, "Be kindly affectioned one to another with brotherly love; in honor preferring one another" (KJV). Your neighborhood and the playground at school are filled with kids from all walks of life. This is especially common in military communities. You will meet children with all kinds of experiences, talents, and gifts. Get to know something about each person you meet.

When we think about Jesus and His friendships, we see that He honored others more than Himself. He honored the people in His community and helped others along the way. Jesus teaches us to honor and love others as He did.

Try to look out for your neighbors, make new friends, and find someone to honor each day.

I will:

_____
_____
_____
_____
_____
_____
_____
_____
_____
_____

Hope-Full

"Rejoice in hope, be patient in tribulation, be constant in prayer."

Romans 12:12 (ESV)

Romans 15:13 says, "Now the God of hope fill you with all joy and peace in believing, that you may abound in hope, through the power of the Holy Ghost" (KJV). Hope is wanting something good to happen when you're not sure how things will turn out.

God want us to put all our confidence in Him. When we have hope, we always expect a great outcome. We believe with confidence that God hears our prayers. Isaiah 55:11 says that the Word of God will not come back empty. It will accomplish what He wants it to accomplish. Place your hope in the Lord, and He will give you the things your heart desires. Our Father knows what is best for us, and He will give us the things that will bring us close to Him.

Hope is big trust in our God. He wants the best for us — to bring us closer to Him.

I will:

_____
_____
_____
_____
_____
_____
_____
_____
_____
_____
_____
_____
_____

Integrity Is Key

"Whoever walks in integrity walks securely, but he who makes his ways crooked will be found out."

Proverbs 10:9 (ESV)

As we discussed earlier, speak the truth from your heart so you can enjoy God's presence (Psalm 15:1–2). Integrity is sometimes summed up as "doing the right thing, even when no one is looking." Integrity is closely related to honesty. You will have nothing to fear or regret when you walk in honesty and truth according to God's Word and the values and morals your parents taught you.

Hiding the truth takes a lot of work; you have to figure out how to continue the same story with each lie. God doesn't want us to stumble by lying, cheating on our tests, etc. He says to cast our cares on Him. He wants us to live free from the cares of this world, honor Him, and follow His Word as the example He has set before us.

Pray that you will walk in honesty and keep walking that way. Put one foot in front of another, trust God for direction, and ask Him for wisdom and knowledge as you deal with things at school and in your life. Stay on the straight path God has set before you, knowing He has a plan and a purpose just for you.

I will:

_____
_____
_____
_____
_____
_____
_____

Joy Unspeakable

"A joyful heart is good medicine, but a crushed spirit dries up the bones."

Proverbs 17:22 (ESV)

Jesus Others Yourself — **JOY**

In Genesis 21:6, we see that Sarah laughed when God told her she would give birth to a son named Isaac. She thought it was a joke, but it was a true and joyful blessing from God. God's Word says that the joy of the Lord is our strength (Nehemiah 8:10). We must trust God in all our situations because it is always joyful to belong to the Lord.

Remember that joy and happiness are totally different. Happiness is temporary, but joy remains with us regardless of our circumstances. Joy is one of the fruits of the Spirit that we produce because God works in us. God has great things in store for everyone, including children.

Think about the things that bring you joy.

I will:

_____
_____
_____
_____
_____
_____
_____
_____
_____
_____
_____

Love

"My command is this: Love each other as I have loved you."

John 15:12 (NIV)

Love is the foundation of life. When Jesus was asked about the greatest commandment, he responded, "'Love the Lord your God with all your heart and with all your soul and with all your mind.' This is the first and greatest commandment. And the second is like it: 'Love your neighbor as yourself.' All the Law and the Prophets hang on these two commandments" (Matthew 22:37–40 NIV).

Even though he was known as a sinful tax collector, Zacchaeus wanted to see Jesus the day He came to town. This story in Luke 19:1–10 helps us understand that unkind, unpleasant, unlovable people still want to be known and loved, even though they don't act like it. Jesus gave a wonderful example in this story of reaching out to someone who was unloved by many. He went out of His way to reach out, and Zacchaeus' heart was changed by that love.

We are chosen out of this world to bear fruit. God created His love for us by dying on the cross. The love of God is more than an emotion or feeling. We experience it through the work of the Holy Spirit in our lives. This reminds us of God's love every day.

I will:

_____
_____
_____
_____
_____
_____
_____
_____

Obedience

"Children, obey your parents in everything, for this pleases the Lord."

Colossians 3:20 (NIV)

Being obedient to God is very important. We should also be obedient to other people in authority like our parents and teachers.

Sometimes everything in us wants to rebel against what we're told to do. Sometimes you may not want to follow your parents' instructions when they ask you to clean your room, stay away from bad company, get your homework done, etc. However, in Christ, we must be changed — transformed (Romans 12:1-2).

This isn't an easy task, but it can be done. If you feel rebellious today, put that feeling at Jesus' feet and ask Him to change your heart and help you be obedient. Obedience is an important lesson that we should learn as early as possible.

Jesus was the perfect model of humility and obedience. He did everything His Father wanted Him to do by dying on the cross to save us from our sins. He wanted to please God so His work could be finished. We must look for the obstacles in our lives that are keeping us from being obedient. Step out in faith and surround yourself with people who will be an encouragement to you and not discourage you from what God has planned for your life.

I will:

_____
_____
_____
_____
_____
_____
_____

Praise Is What We Do

"We proclaim how great you are and tell of the wonderful things you have done."

Psalm 75:1 (NIV)

Praise and worship aren't something we naturally want to do, but they usually make us feel better in the toughest times. Whenever we praise and worship God, things happen in our lives. Try praising Him before you take a test or go to school. Praise changes the atmosphere and our attitudes.

Nothing is more powerful and life changing than praise and worship and giving God glory and honor for all He has done. When you are struggling with your attitude, praise God and think on His goodness. When you do, watch the atmosphere and your attitude change.

You can praise God in many ways. One way is to sing in the spirit with instruments. You can also praise God by sharing His wonderful works with others, telling them of His endless love, mercy, and grace.

I will:

_____
_____
_____
_____
_____
_____
_____
_____
_____
_____
_____
_____

Be Passionate

"But seek first his kingdom and his righteousness, and all these things will be given to you as well."

Matthew 6:33 (NIV)

Do you have a passion? Do you have a strong feeling about something? Do you enjoy life and embrace it with your whole heart? Do you love the Lord with all that is within you?

Try to appreciate life itself. Enjoy every detail of God's creation (Psalm 8). Rejoice in the small things in life, as well as the big things. Sit back and look at how amazing God's creation is. Seek new things in life as a young child, and never let it be a chore or burden. Laugh more and rejoice in the Lord always (Philippians 4:4). Be passionate about your faith and your love for God. Passion involves hard work and the willingness to accept failure. Having passion will make you feel like you have a purpose in life.

Stay connected to your most important plan — your destiny. In the moments that you struggle, remember that God knows the plan and purpose He has for you (Jeremiah 29:11). Surrender your dreams and gifts to God and ask Him to show you what you need to do for Him.

I will:

_____
_____
_____
_____
_____
_____
_____
_____
_____
_____

Peer Pressure

"Do not conform to the pattern of this world, but be transformed by the renewing of your mind. Then you will be able to test and approve what God's will is — his good, pleasing, and perfect will."

Romans 12:2 (NIV)

Your peers influence your life just by spending time with you. You learn from them, and they learn from you. It's human nature to listen to and learn from others, especially those in your age group. It's natural to want to fit in with a group — to feel part of something bigger than yourself.

However, guard your heart and listen to God and His direction (Proverbs 3:6) when you find yourself in the wrong situations. At those very times, it's the hardest to resist peer pressure, but you must still say "No." Sometimes peers influence each other in negative ways. Kids in school might try to get you to cut classes with them, your soccer friend might try to convince you to be mean to another player, kids in the neighborhood might want you to do drugs with them, or some friends might try to get you to shoplift with them. Some kids give in to peer pressure because they want to be popular.

To help you know the right things to do, pay attention to your own feelings and beliefs and the values you have been taught about what is right and wrong. Inner strength and self-confidence can help you stand firm, walk away, and resist doing something you know is wrong. Don't be afraid — God will be with you (Joshua 1:9).

I will:

_____
_____
_____
_____
_____
_____

Perseverance

"Consider it pure joy, my brothers and sisters, whenever you face trials of many kinds, because you know that the testing of your faith produces perseverance. Let perseverance finish its work so that you may be mature and complete, not lacking anything."

James 1:2-4 (NIV)

Perseverance is the ability to get through difficult tasks. When things don't go as planned, how do we get back up and go at them again? So how do we learn this important skill? Perseverance can be inborn, but in most of us, it needs to be cultivated and nurtured.

Perseverance means not giving up. It keeps you going when you want to quit. In math, science, reading, or any subject, it can be hard to just stay focused. If you play sports, you know that to persevere means you push yourself beyond a big wall that sits in front of you. You must break down the things you thought would limit you.

Keep your eyes on the prize, which is the Lord. Run the race with patience and don't give up. When you cross that finish line, you will run into the arms of Jesus, the author and finisher of our faith (Hebrews 12:1-2). When you pray, ask Him to help you through tough times you may have in school — perhaps with peer pressure or playground troubles, but mostly in the race called life.

I will:
_____
_____
_____
_____
_____
_____
_____

Prayer — the Game Changer

"But thou, when thou prayest, enter into thy closet, and when thou hast shut thy door, pray to thy Father which is in secret; and thy Father which seeth in secret shall reward thee openly."

Matthew 6:6 (KJV)

Learning to pray is an essential part of knowing Jesus and supporting your relationships with God. Our Lord gave us prayer, so we could communicate with Him directly, and being comfortable with prayer helps you understand God is always close when you need Him. Prayer is a powerful tool, and if you learn to use it while you are young, you will likely pray throughout your whole life.

Prayer journaling is a great way to learn how to pray. Purchase or make prayer journals out of notebook or. Write down prayers, as well as thoughts and feelings. Make notes when prayers have been answered. God loves for us to communicate with Him. We can't go wrong talking to God. He loves quality time.

Family prayer times are very important, as they involve much love and devotion. Pray for your family, friends, the body of Christ, the hurt, the lost, the lonely, the afflicted, schools, teachers, grandparents, and so on. Ask your parents to do a regular family prayer time and know that your prayers are powerful and will change lives — starting with yours.

I will:

_____
_____
_____
_____
_____
_____
_____

Respect

"Be devoted to one another in love. Honor one another above yourselves."

Romans 12:10 (NIV)

Respect is a big concept to grasp as a kid. Respect includes how you feel about people and how you treat them. Having respect for people means you think good things about them and show a friendly attitude toward them.

When you are respectful, you show people that you accept them for who they are, as well as their differences. You may show special respect to certain people because of their color, their backgrounds, the fact that they have special needs, etc. Showing respect means you honor others above yourself. Respect doesn't necessarily come naturally, but it is very important that you learn it.

Not only did God create us and design plans for us, but He calls us to value, cherish, and guard human life because it is sacred. We must respect and pray for others as Jesus did.

I will:

_____
_____
_____
_____
_____
_____
_____
_____
_____
_____
_____
_____

Self-Control

"Be ye angry, and sin not: let not the sun go down upon your wrath: Neither give place to the devil."

Ephesians 4:26–27 (KJV)

By learning self-control, you can make the right decisions, even when you are stressed out. Because we face many decisions every day, we need to have self-control in our attitudes toward others, especially when we disagree with them. We need to maintain healthy boundaries that help us control our thoughts and attitudes.

As we see in Galatians 5:22, self-control is a fruit of the Spirit. The wonderful thing is that we do not have to be controlled by our own desires or whims. We are not weak but strong in Christ. Think about the areas in which you need to practice self-control. Write them down and pray about them. You don't have to let these sinful patterns control your life. The Holy Spirit gives you the power to break free.

I will:

_____
_____
_____
_____
_____
_____
_____
_____
_____
_____
_____
_____
_____

Live Selflessly

"Anyone who loves their life will lose it, while anyone who hates their life in this world will keep it for eternal life."

John 12:25 (NIV)

It is our nature to be selfish — to want others to serve us rather than to be servants ourselves. Being filled with the Holy Spirit affects the way we live daily. It changes our attitudes and actions. Such an attitude of praise and gratitude compels us not only to serve God but to change our attitude toward serving others.

"If anyone serves me, he must follow me; and where I am, there will my servant be also. If anyone serves me, the Father will honor him" (John 12:26 ESV). Think about the attitudes Jesus expressed. Being fully human, Jesus experienced natural feelings like we do. He felt grief at the thought of dying on the cross.

God has something for each of us to do, and some things may require sacrifice. However, dying to self may become merely good works if God isn't calling you to make those sacrifices. He wants you to focus more on Him than on yourself. Selfless service demands that you consider the needs of others.

Take the time to esteem others more than yourself. Think about how you can help others in your church and consider the gifts and passions the Lord has placed inside of you. Look for ways you can use them to bring God glory.

I will:

_____
_____
_____
_____
_____
_____

Thankfulness

"I will praise the name of God with a song; I will magnify Him with thanksgiving."

Psalm 69:30 (ESV)

Thanksgiving Day is a time to reflect and be thankful for all God has given us. God deserves our thankfulness. When someone gives or sends you a gift in the mail, you should either write a thank-you card or give him or her a call. God wants us to give thanks in all things. He wants us to trust that He will provide great outcomes, then give thanks when He does.

In the following story, we see that Jesus healed ten lepers. Notice how many took the time to say, "Thank you": "And as he entered a village, he was met by ten lepers, who stood at a distance and lifted their voices, saying, 'Jesus, Master, have mercy on us.' When he saw them he said to them, 'Go and show yourselves to the priests.' And as they went they were cleansed. Then one of them, when he saw that he was healed, turned back, praising God with a loud voice; and he fell on his face at Jesus' feet, giving him thanks. Now he was a Samaritan. Then Jesus answered, 'Were not ten cleansed? Where are the nine? Was no one found to return and give praise to God except this foreigner?' And he said to him, 'Rise and go your way; your faith has made you well'" (**Luke 17:12–19 ESV**).

I will:

_____
_____
_____
_____
_____
_____
_____
_____

Trust Him

"Trust in the Lord with all your heart and lean not on your own understanding."

Proverbs 3:5 (NIV)

Why do bad things happen to good people? We've all asked that question at one time or another. The answer is that all things work together for our good (Romans 8:28). Trust God in everything; He doesn't make mistakes. He has proven that He can help us no matter where we are. He is everything to us.

We are called to trust God during all times — the good and the bad. The best example of this is found in the book of Job. Sometimes it's tough to trust God, but He wants us to learn that even though we don't understand why He allows bad things to happen, He is always in control.

Difficult times are all too real, and we find it hard to trust God in these unwanted situations. We must get to know God and know that we can confidently trust Him to protect us. Psalm 91:4 says, "He will cover you with his feathers, and under his wings you will find refuge; his faithfulness will be your shield and rampart" (NIV).

I will:

_____
_____
_____
_____
_____
_____
_____
_____
_____
_____

Values

"Listen, my son, to your father's instruction and do not forsake your mother's teaching. They are a garland to grace your head and a chain to adorn your neck."

Proverbs 1:8–9 (NIV)

Respect, kindness, honesty, courage, perseverance, self-discipline, compassion, generosity, dependability, honesty, trust. Your parents teach you these values to protect you from bad influences and help you become good citizens. You may consider clothing, shoes, toys, and other things as valuable. However, God wants you to focus on spiritual things.

Philippians 4:8 says, "Finally, brethren, whatsoever things are true, whatsoever things are honest, whatsoever things are just, whatsoever things are pure, whatsoever things are lovely, whatsoever things are of good report; if there be any virtue, and if there be any praise, think on these things" (KJV).

God is not impressed by name-brand clothing or shoes. He is impressed by the love He sees in your heart toward Him and others. He is impressed when you speak honest words and live according to His Word. Sit down and think about the most valuable thing you have to offer God.

I will:

_____
_____
_____
_____
_____
_____
_____
_____
_____

Wisdom

"For we are his workmanship, created in Christ Jesus for good works, which God prepared beforehand, that we should walk in them."

Ephesians 2:10 (ESV)

The book of Proverbs offers much great wisdom. James 1:5 tell us to ask God for wisdom. There are two kinds of wisdom — worldly wisdom and godly wisdom. Fearing God means that we honor, revere, worship, obey, serve, and respect Him.

Fearing God also means that we do not want to displease Him. We are afraid of sin's consequences and doing the things God says are evil, wrong, hurtful, or dishonoring to Him and to others. Don't be intimidated by what others think and say. Trust in God's wisdom. Everything He does is for your good. Trust Him in everything. If you ask for wisdom, He will give it to you. He cannot wait to share His heart with you.

I will:
___
___
___
___
___
___
___
___
___
___
___
___
___
___
___

About the Author

Lorraine Jones Whitfield is the wife of Elder Carlton Whitfield, Sr. Lorraine is dedicated to helping people live according to God's Word and walk in the purposes to which God has called them. She mentors, coaches, and consults in a marriage and family ministry and a children's ministry. She is also a Christian life coach. She is the CEO of Hannah's Heart Ministry and SHE Soars LLC.

Women have been blessed by Lorraine's online women's book ministry, her marriage and family ministry, and her ability to lead and guide hurting women by equipping, educating, encouraging, and empowering. She does this through the Word of God and other resources, such as women's prayer breakfasts, women's empowerment and transformational sessions, and her anointed individual training (AIT) boot camps. She seeks to help women WIN (walk in new). She is available to speak at your women's events, as well.

Lorraine and Carlton have been married for more than 35 years. The parents of 7 and grandparents of 14, they reside in Wilson, North Carolina, where together they work in the ministry. Carlton is a pastor and currently mentors and instructs in God's Word with an awesome online ministry and home-based Bible study group. Lorraine and Carlton love to meet people where they are and reach them for God's glory.

www.lorrainejoneswhitfield.com
https://www.shesoarsllc.com
https://www.facebook.com/lorraine.whitfield
email: **hannahsheart7@gmail.com**

Made in the USA
Middletown, DE
21 November 2021